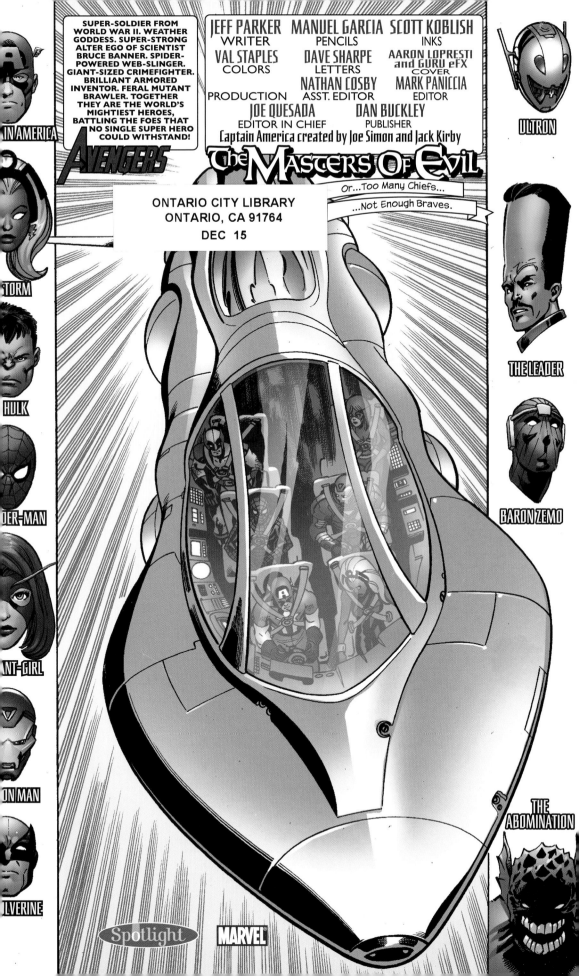

SUPER-SOLDIER FROM WORLD WAR II. WEATHER GODDESS. SUPER-STRONG ALTER EGO OF SCIENTIST BRUCE BANNER. SPIDER-POWERED WEB-SLINGER. GIANT-SIZED CRIMEFIGHTER. BRILLIANT ARMORED INVENTOR. FERAL MUTANT BRAWLER. TOGETHER THEY ARE THE WORLD'S MIGHTIEST HEROES, BATTLING THE FOES THAT NO SINGLE SUPER HERO COULD WITHSTAND!

JEFF PARKER
WRITER

MANUEL GARCIA
PENCILS

SCOTT KOBLISH
INKS

VAL STAPLES
COLORS

DAVE SHARPE
LETTERS

AARON LOPRESTI and GURU eFX
COVER

PRODUCTION

NATHAN COSBY
ASST. EDITOR

MARK PANICCIA
EDITOR

JOE QUESADA
EDITOR IN CHIEF

DAN BUCKLEY
PUBLISHER

Captain America created by Joe Simon and Jack Kirby

AVENGERS

THE MASTERS OF EVIL

Or...Too Many Chiefs...

...Not Enough Braves.

IN AMERICA

STORM

HULK

DER-MAN

NT-GIRL

ON MAN

LVERINE

ULTRON

THE LEADER

BARON ZEMO

THE ABOMINATION

Spotlight

MARVEL

VISIT US AT
www.abdopublishing.com

Reinforced library bound edition published in 2008 by Spotlight, a division of the ABDO Publishing
Group, 8000 West 78th Street, Edina, Minnesota 55439. Spotlight produces high-quality reinforced
library bound editions for schools and libraries. Published by agreement with Marvel Characters, Inc.

Printed in the United States of America, North Mankato, Minnesota.
012007 072013

Library of Congress Cataloging-in-Publication Data

Parker, Jeff, 1966-
  The masters of evil / Jeff Parker, writer ; Manuel Garcia, penciler ; Scott Koblish, inker ; Val Staples,
colorist ; Dave Sharpe, letterer ; Aaron Lopresti and GURU eFX, cover. -- Reinforced library bound ed.
      p. cm. -- (The Avengers)
  "Marvel age"--Cover.
  Revision of issue 4 of Marvel adventures, the Avengers.
  ISBN 978-1-59961-385-7
  1. Graphic novels. I. Garcia, Manuel. II. Marvel adventures, the Avengers. 4. III. Title.

PN6728.A94P35 2008
741.5'973--dc22

                                                                    2007020246

All Spotlight books have reinforced library bindings
and are manufactured in the United States of America.

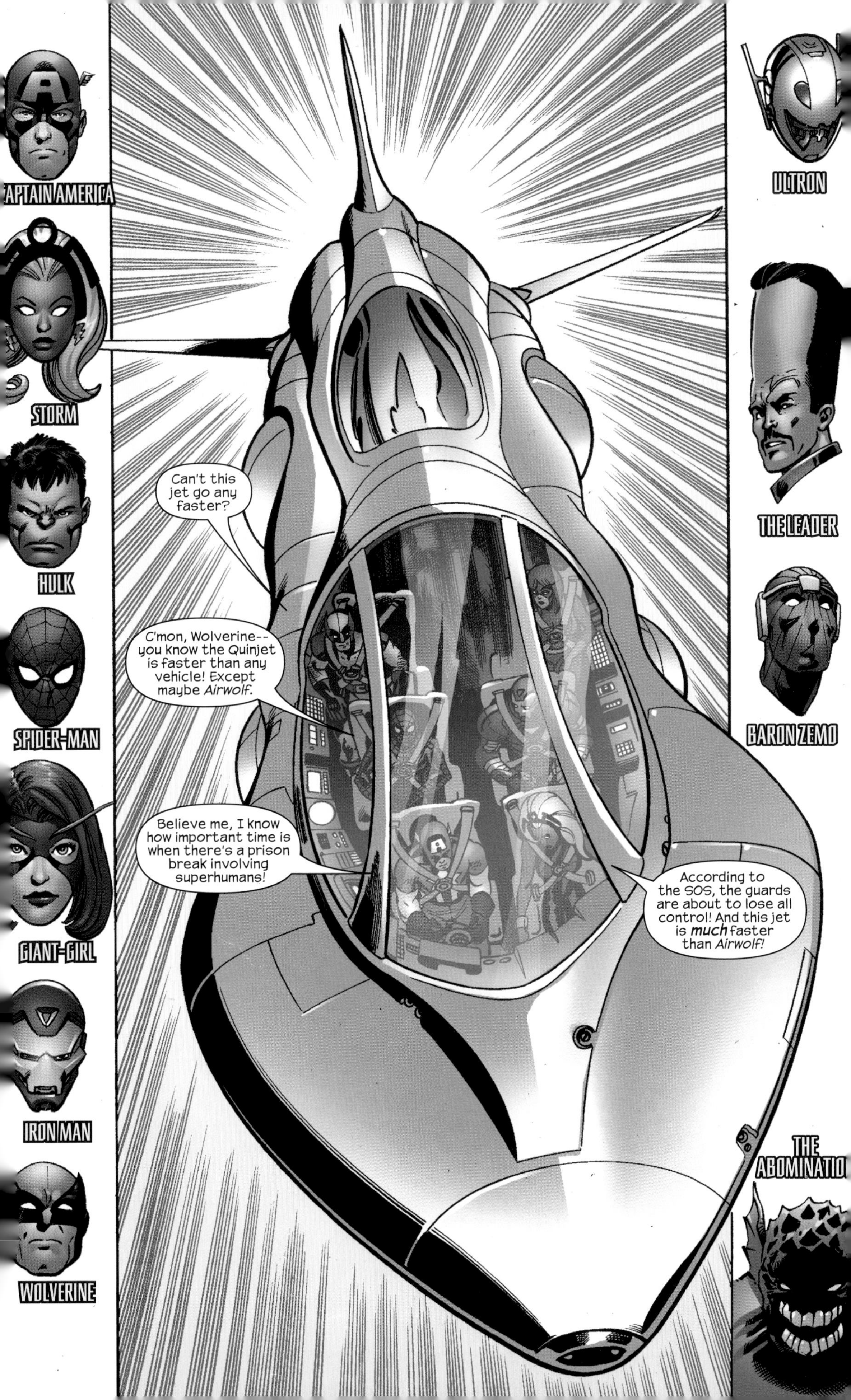
CAPTAIN AMERICA
STORM
HULK
SPIDER-MAN
GIANT-GIRL
IRON MAN
WOLVERINE
ULTRON
THE LEADER
BARON ZEMO
THE ABOMINATIO
Can't this jet go any faster?
C'mon, Wolverine-- you know the Quinjet is faster than any vehicle! Except maybe *Airwolf*.
Believe me, I know how important time is when there's a prison break involving superhumans!
According to the SOS, the guards are about to lose all control! And this jet is ***much*** faster than *Airwolf*!

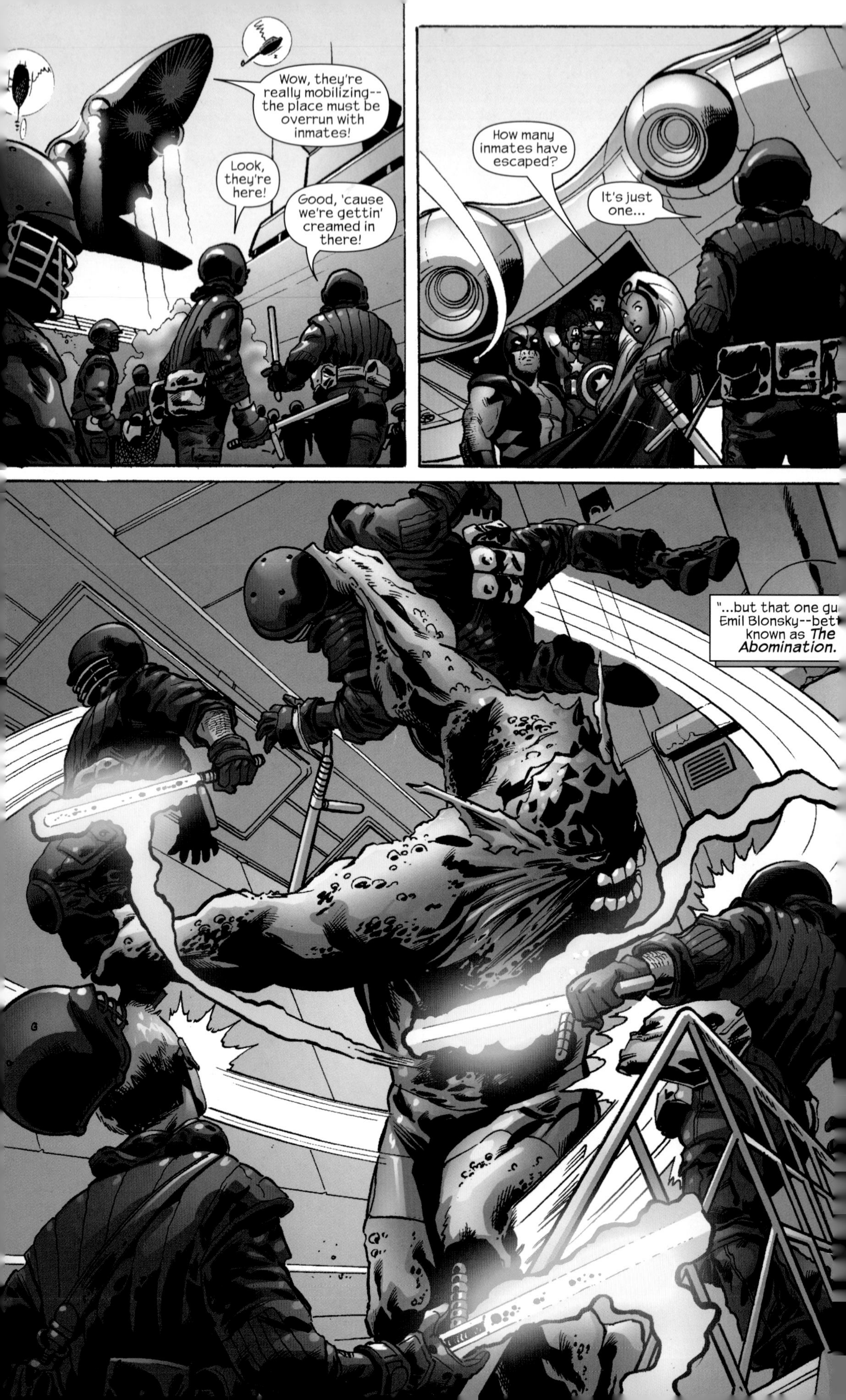
Wow, they're really mobilizing--the place must be overrun with inmates!
Look, they're here!
Good, 'cause we're gettin' creamed in there!
How many inmates have escaped?
It's just one...
"...but that one gu
Emil Blonsky--bett
known as *The Abomination.*

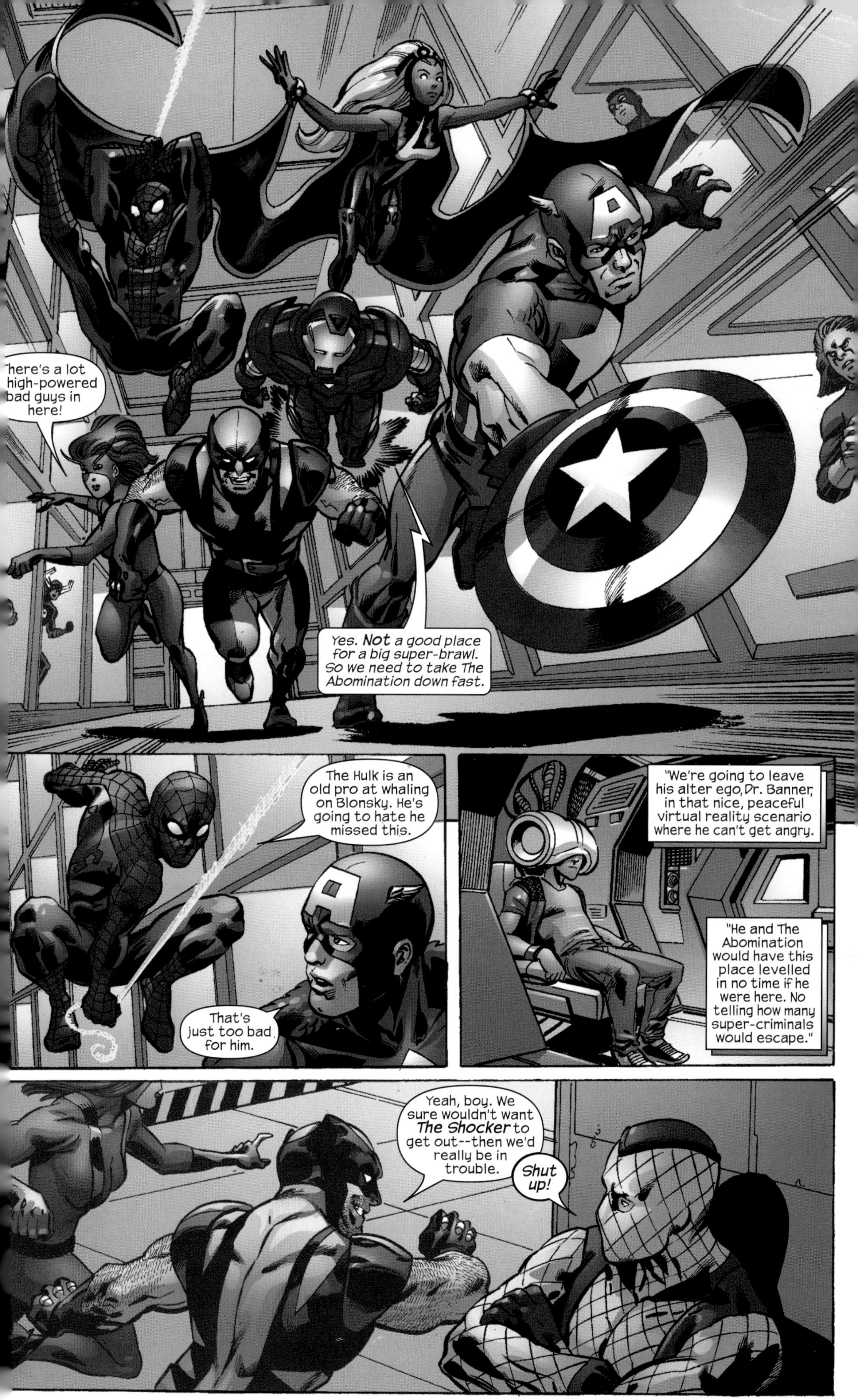
here's a lot
high-powered
bad guys in
here!
Yes. Not a good place for a big super-brawl. So we need to take The Abomination down fast.
The Hulk is an old pro at whaling on Blonsky. He's going to hate he missed this.
That's just too bad for him.
"We're going to leave his alter ego, Dr. Banner, in that nice, peaceful virtual reality scenario where he can't get angry.
"He and The Abomination would have this place levelled in no time if he were here. No telling how many super-criminals would escape."
Yeah, boy. We sure wouldn't want The Shocker to get out--then we'd really be in trouble.
Shut up!

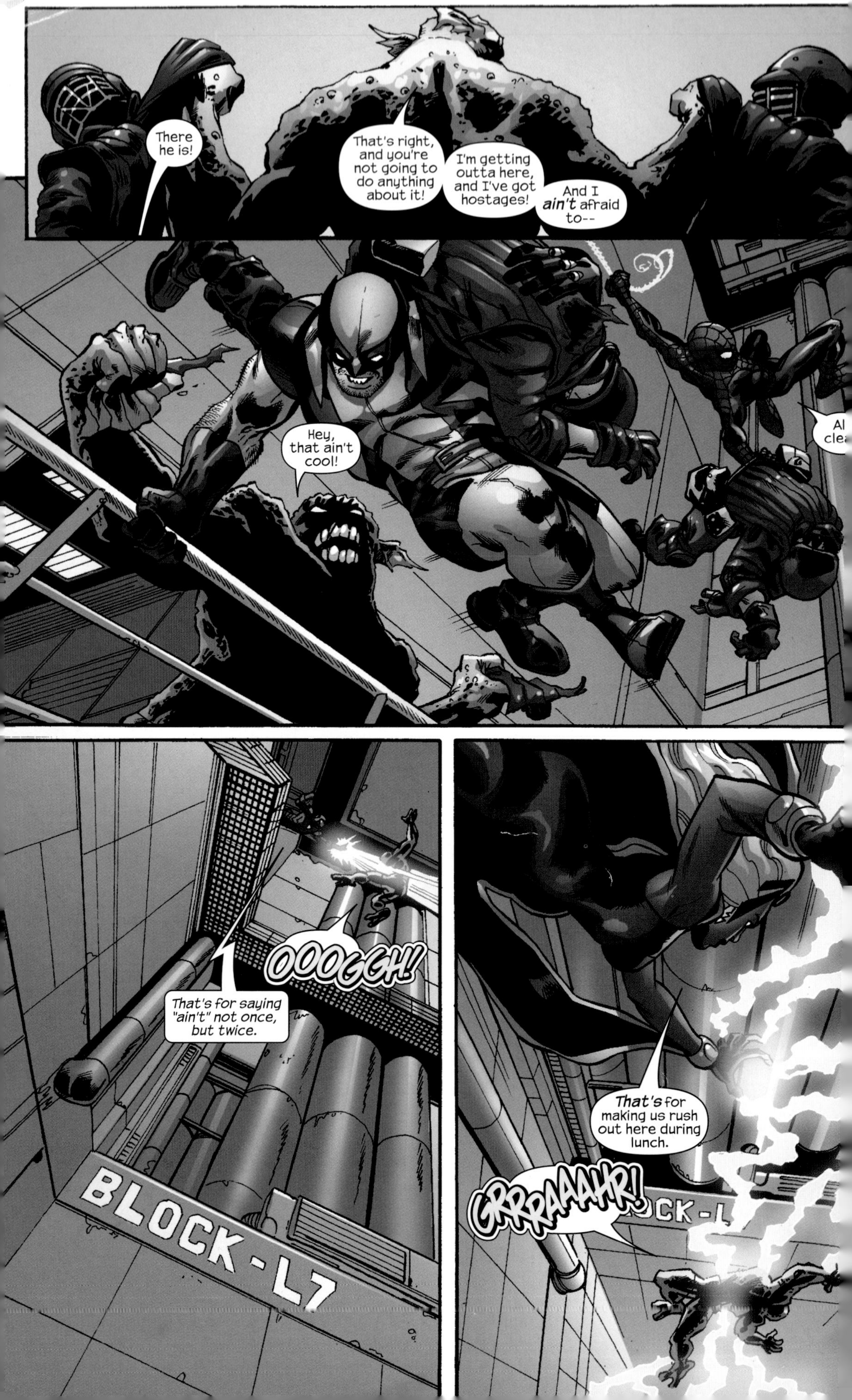
There he is!
That's right, and you're not going to do anything about it!
I'm getting outta here, and I've got hostages!
And I *ain't* afraid to--
Hey, that ain't cool!
OOOGGH!
That's for saying "ain't" not once, but twice.
BLOCK-L7
That's for making us rush out here during lunch.
GRRRAAAHR!

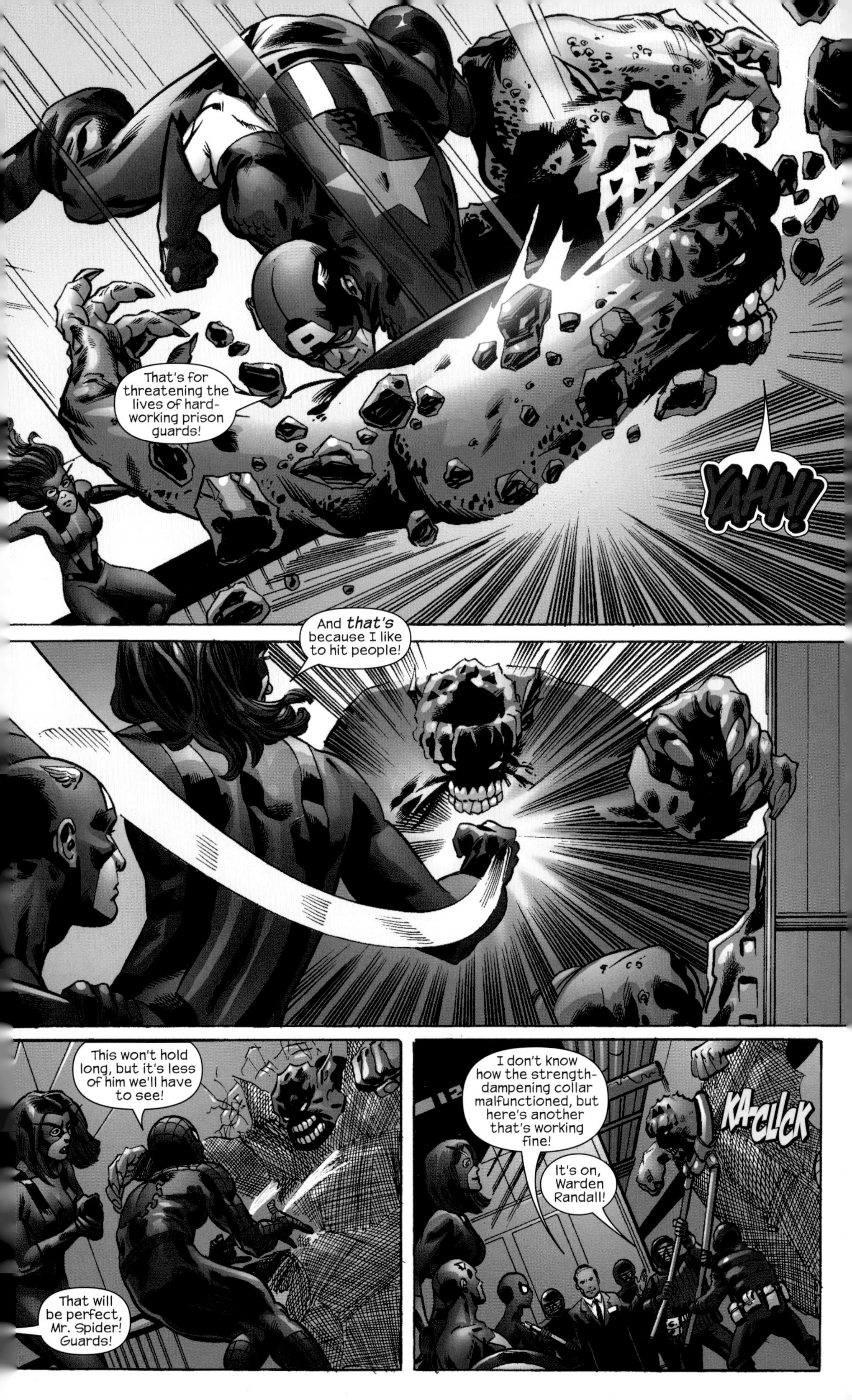
That's for threatening the lives of hard-working prison guards!
YAHH!
And that's because I like to hit people!
This won't hold long, but it's less of him we'll have to see!
That will be perfect, Mr. Spider! Guards!
I don't know how the strength-dampening collar malfunctioned, but here's another that's working fine!
KA-CLICK
It's on, Warden Randall!

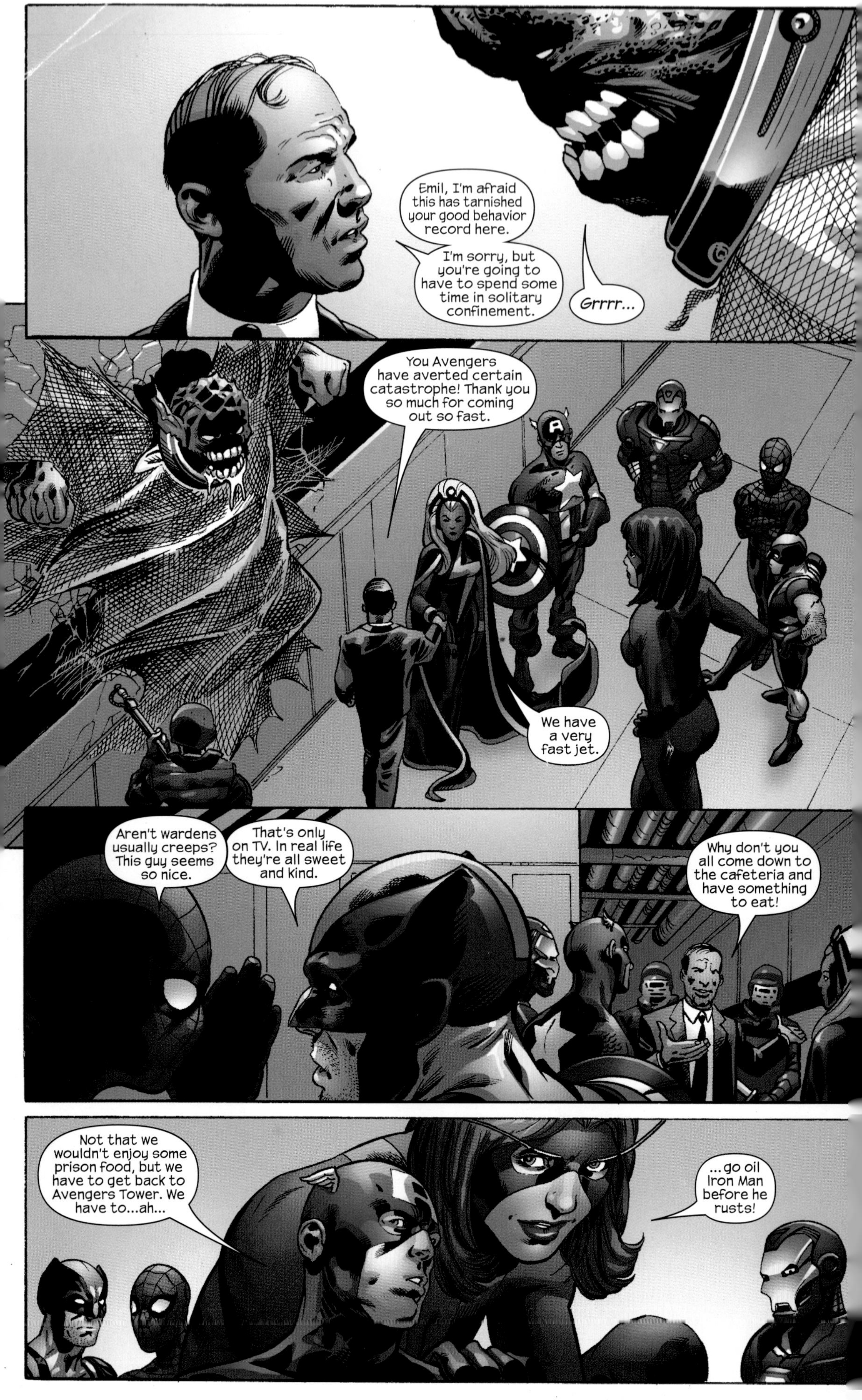
Emil, I'm afraid this has tarnished your good behavior record here.
I'm sorry, but you're going to have to spend some time in solitary confinement.
Grrrr...
You Avengers have averted certain catastrophe! Thank you so much for coming out so fast.
We have a very fast jet.
Aren't wardens usually creeps? This guy seems so nice.
That's only on TV. In real life they're all sweet and kind.
Why don't you all come down to the cafeteria and have something to eat!
Not that we wouldn't enjoy some prison food, but we have to get back to Avengers Tower. We have to...ah...
...go oil Iron Man before he rusts!

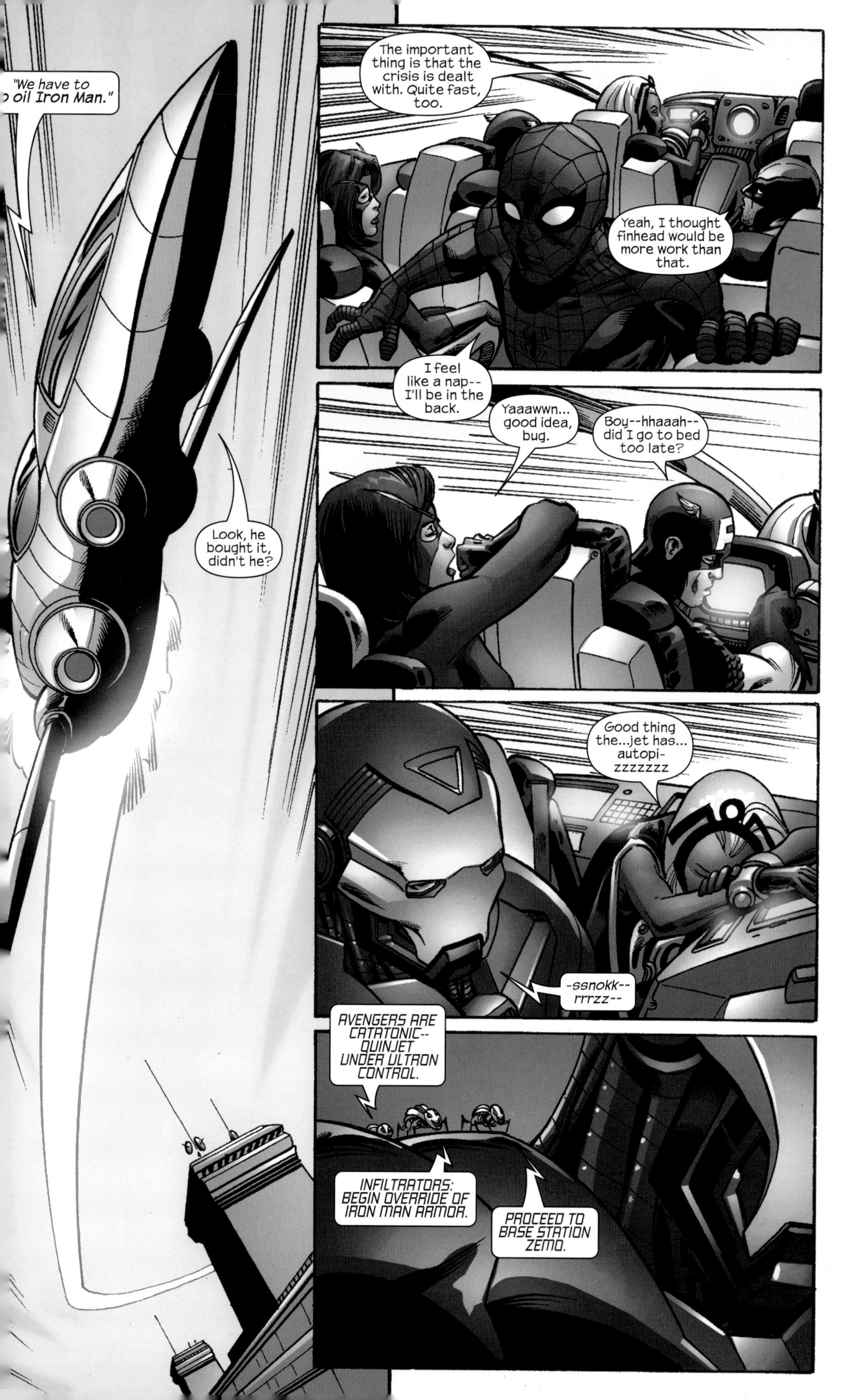
"We have to
o oil Iron Man."
Look, he bought it, didn't he?
The important thing is that the crisis is dealt with. Quite fast, too.
Yeah, I thought finhead would be more work than that.
I feel like a nap--I'll be in the back.
Yaaawwn... good idea, bug.
Boy--hhaaah--did I go to bed too late?
Good thing the...jet has... autopi-zzzzzzz
-ssnokk--rrrzz--
AVENGERS ARE CATATONIC--QUINJET UNDER ULTRON CONTROL.
INFILTRATORS: BEGIN OVERRIDE OF IRON MAN ARMOR.
PROCEED TO BASE STATION ZEMO.

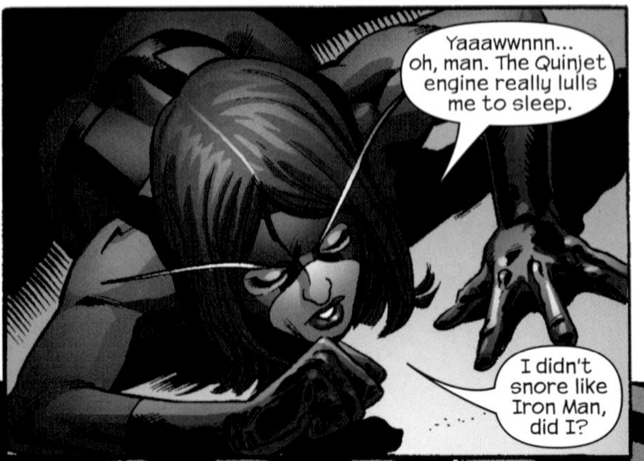
Yaaawwnnn... oh, man. The Quinjet engine really lulls me to sleep.
I didn't snore like Iron Man, did I?

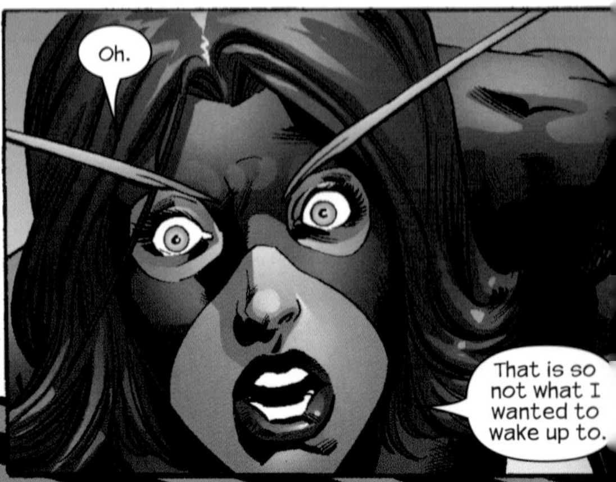
Oh.
That is so not what I wanted to wake up to.

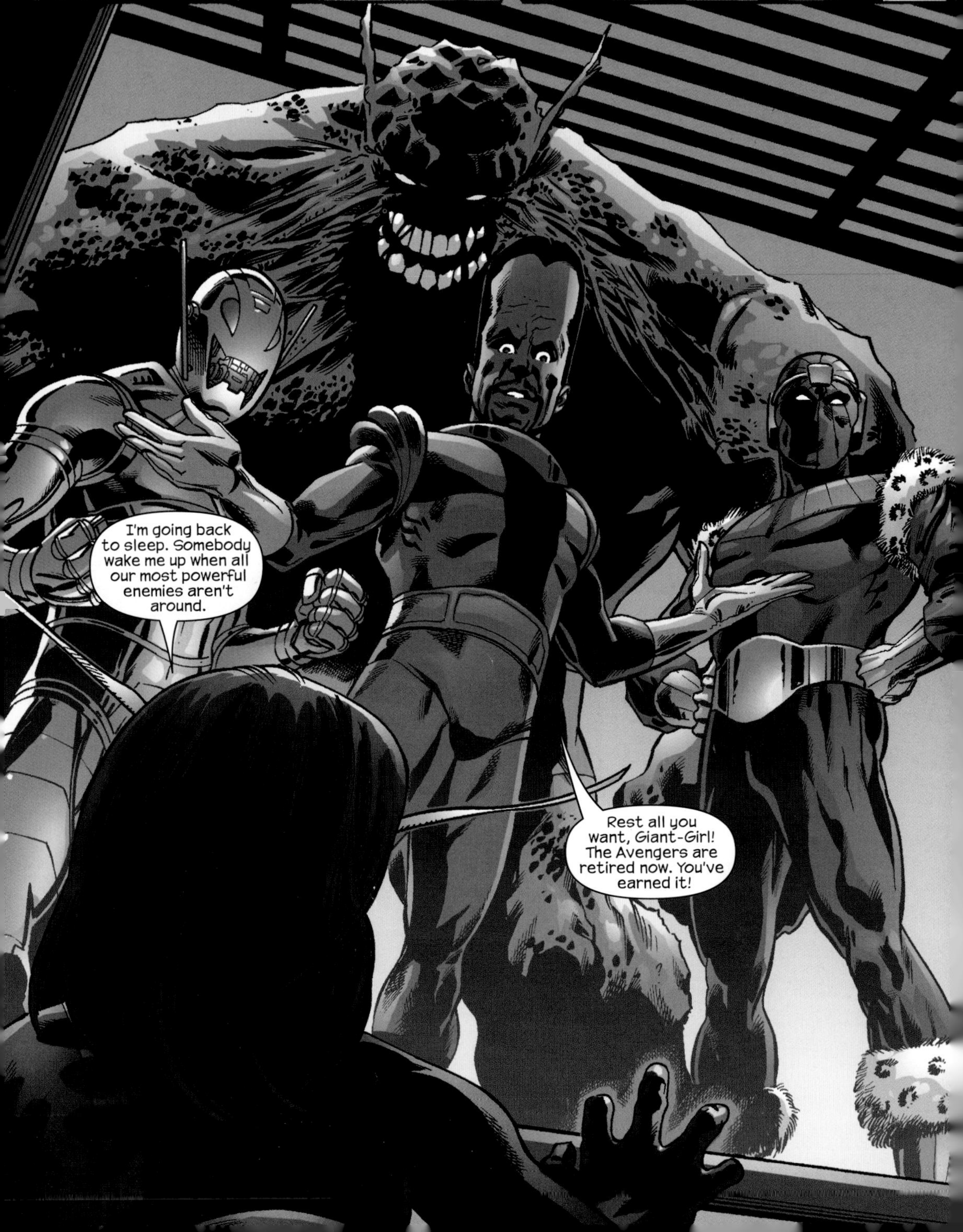
I'm going back to sleep. Somebody wake me up when all our most powerful enemies aren't around.
Rest all you want, Giant-Girl! The Avengers are retired now. You've earned it!

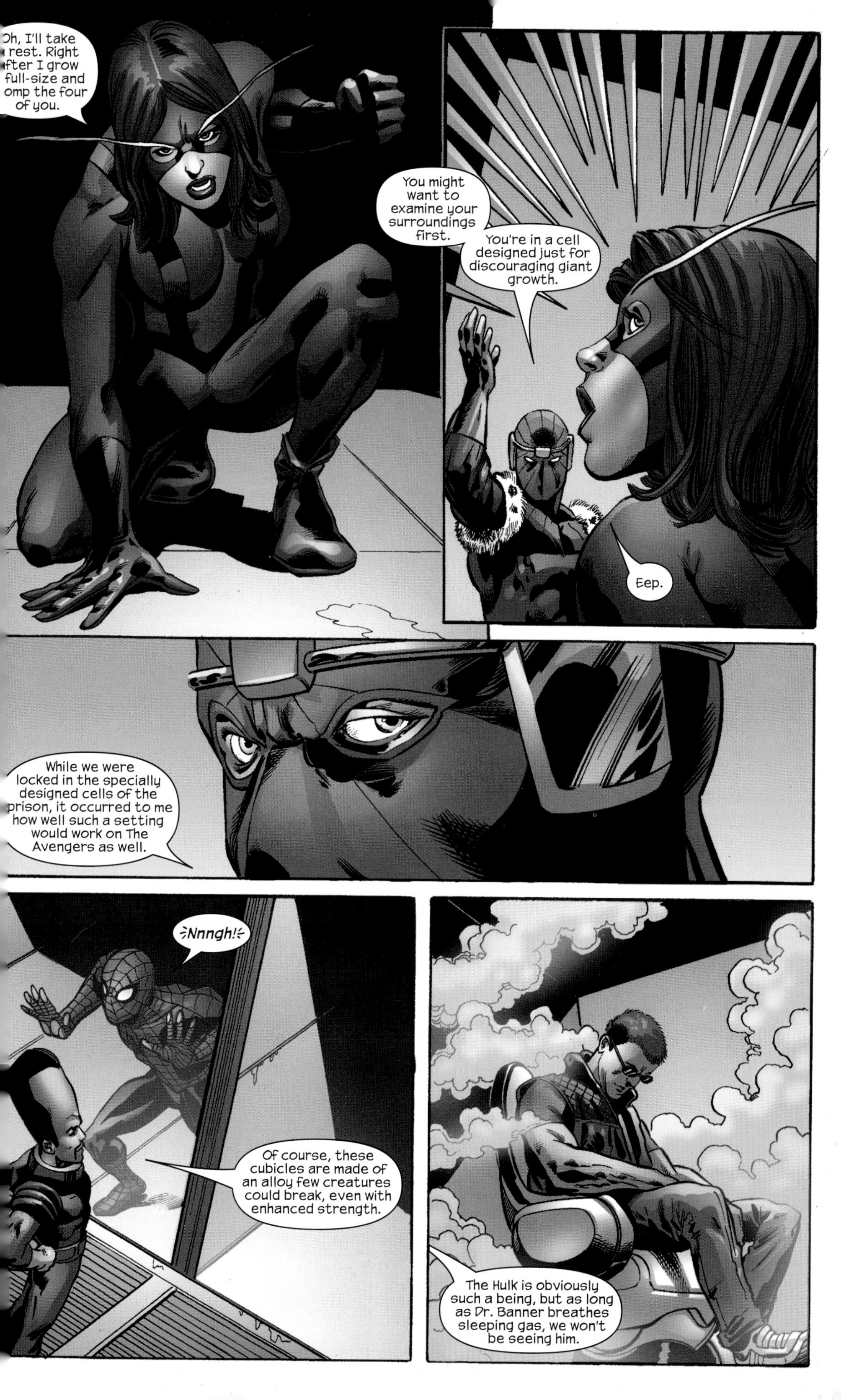

Oh, I'll take
rest. Right
after I grow
full-size and
omp the four
of you.
You might want to examine your surroundings first.
You're in a cell designed just for discouraging giant growth.
Eep.
While we were locked in the specially designed cells of the prison, it occurred to me how well such a setting would work on The Avengers as well.
Nnngh!
Of course, these cubicles are made of an alloy few creatures could break, even with enhanced strength.
The Hulk is obviously such a being, but as long as Dr. Banner breathes sleeping gas, we won't be seeing him.

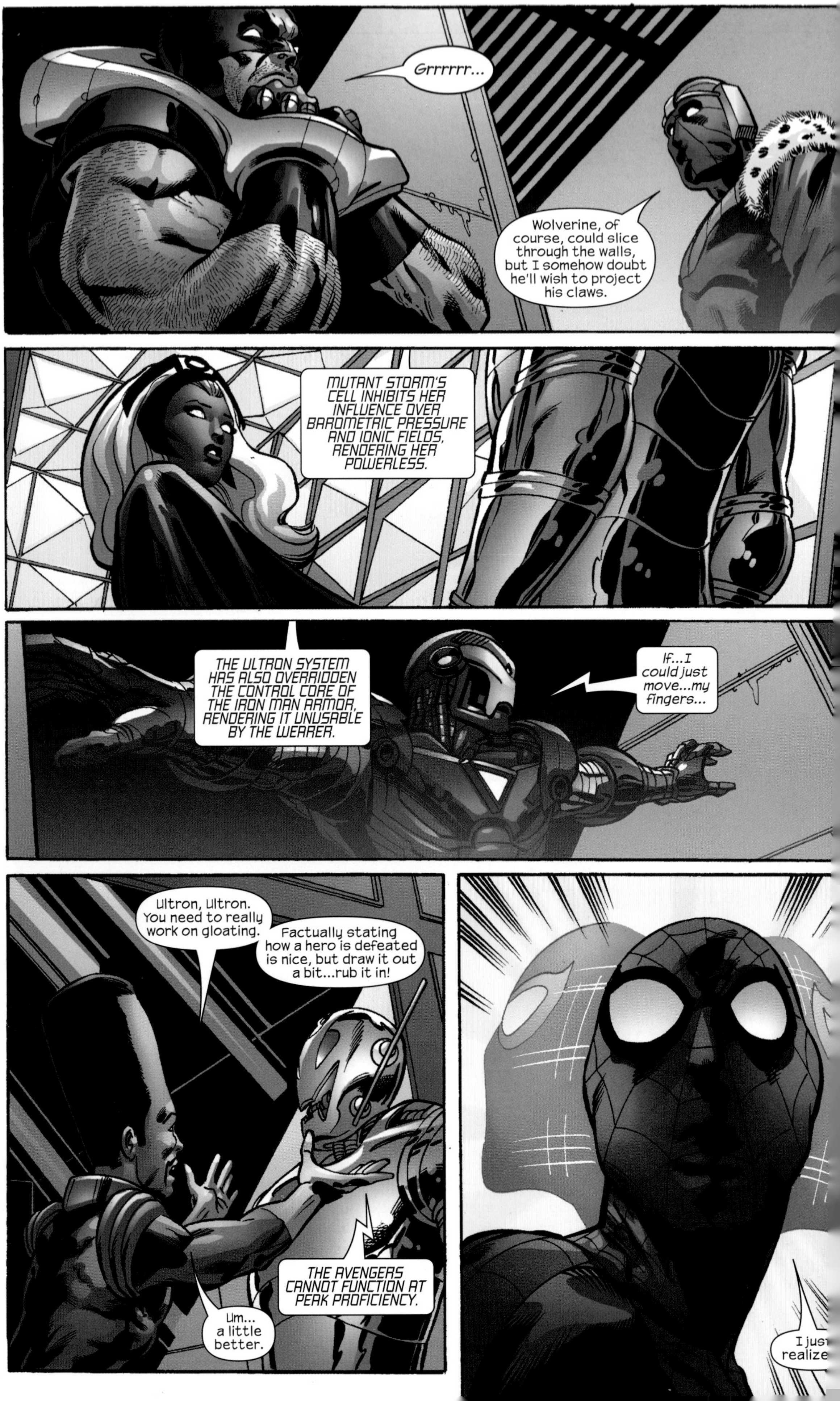
Grrrrrr...
Wolverine, of course, could slice through the walls, but I somehow doubt he'll wish to project his claws.
MUTANT STORM'S CELL INHIBITS HER INFLUENCE OVER BAROMETRIC PRESSURE AND IONIC FIELDS, RENDERING HER POWERLESS.
THE ULTRON SYSTEM HAS ALSO OVERRIDDEN THE CONTROL CORE OF THE IRON MAN ARMOR, RENDERING IT UNUSABLE BY THE WEARER.
If...I could just move...my fingers...
Ultron, Ultron. You need to really work on gloating.
Factually stating how a hero is defeated is nice, but draw it out a bit...rub it in!
THE AVENGERS CANNOT FUNCTION AT PEAK PROFICIENCY.
Um... a little better.

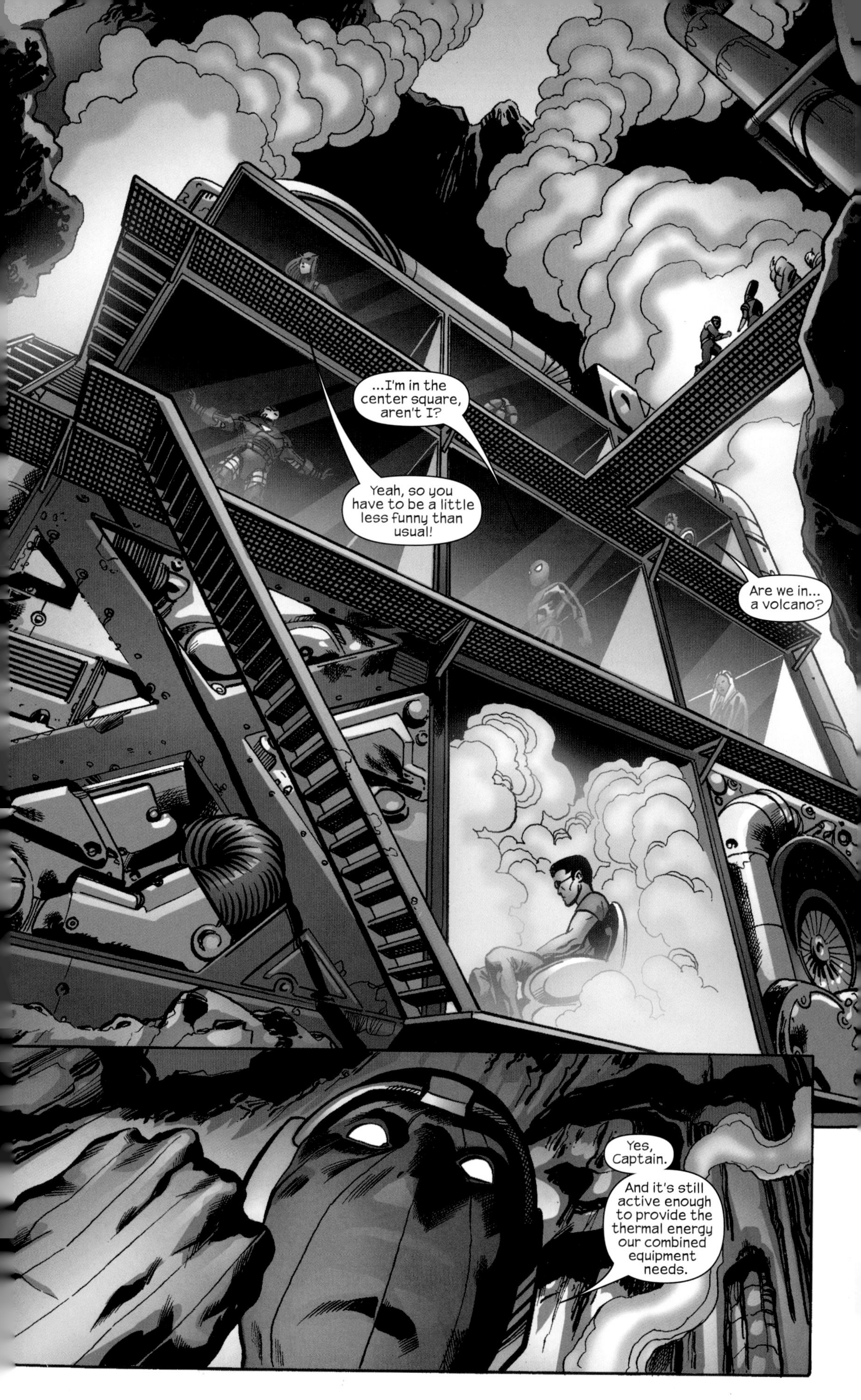
...I'm in the center square, aren't I?
Yeah, so you have to be a little less funny than usual!
Are we in... a volcano?
Yes, Captain.
And it's still active enough to provide the thermal energy our combined equipment needs.

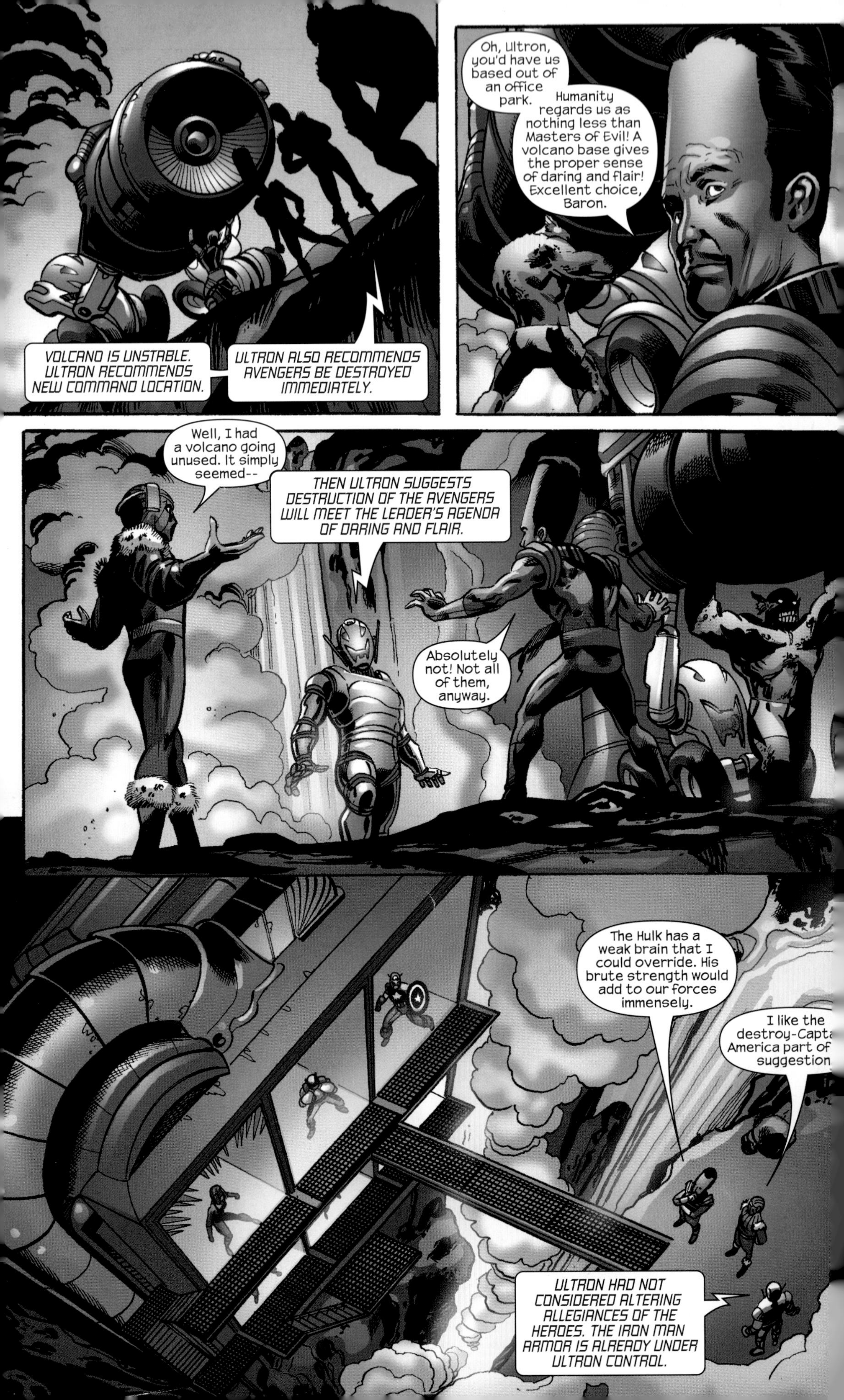
VOLCANO IS UNSTABLE. ULTRON RECOMMENDS NEW COMMAND LOCATION.
ULTRON ALSO RECOMMENDS AVENGERS BE DESTROYED IMMEDIATELY.
Oh, Ultron, you'd have us based out of an office park.
Humanity regards us as nothing less than Masters of Evil! A volcano base gives the proper sense of daring and flair! Excellent choice, Baron.
Well, I had a volcano going unused. It simply seemed--
THEN ULTRON SUGGESTS DESTRUCTION OF THE AVENGERS WILL MEET THE LEADER'S AGENDA OF DARING AND FLAIR.
Absolutely not! Not all of them, anyway.
The Hulk has a weak brain that I could override. His brute strength would add to our forces immensely.
I like the destroy-Capta America part of suggestion
ULTRON HAD NOT CONSIDERED ALTERING ALLEGIANCES OF THE HEROES. THE IRON MAN ARMOR IS ALREADY UNDER ULTRON CONTROL.

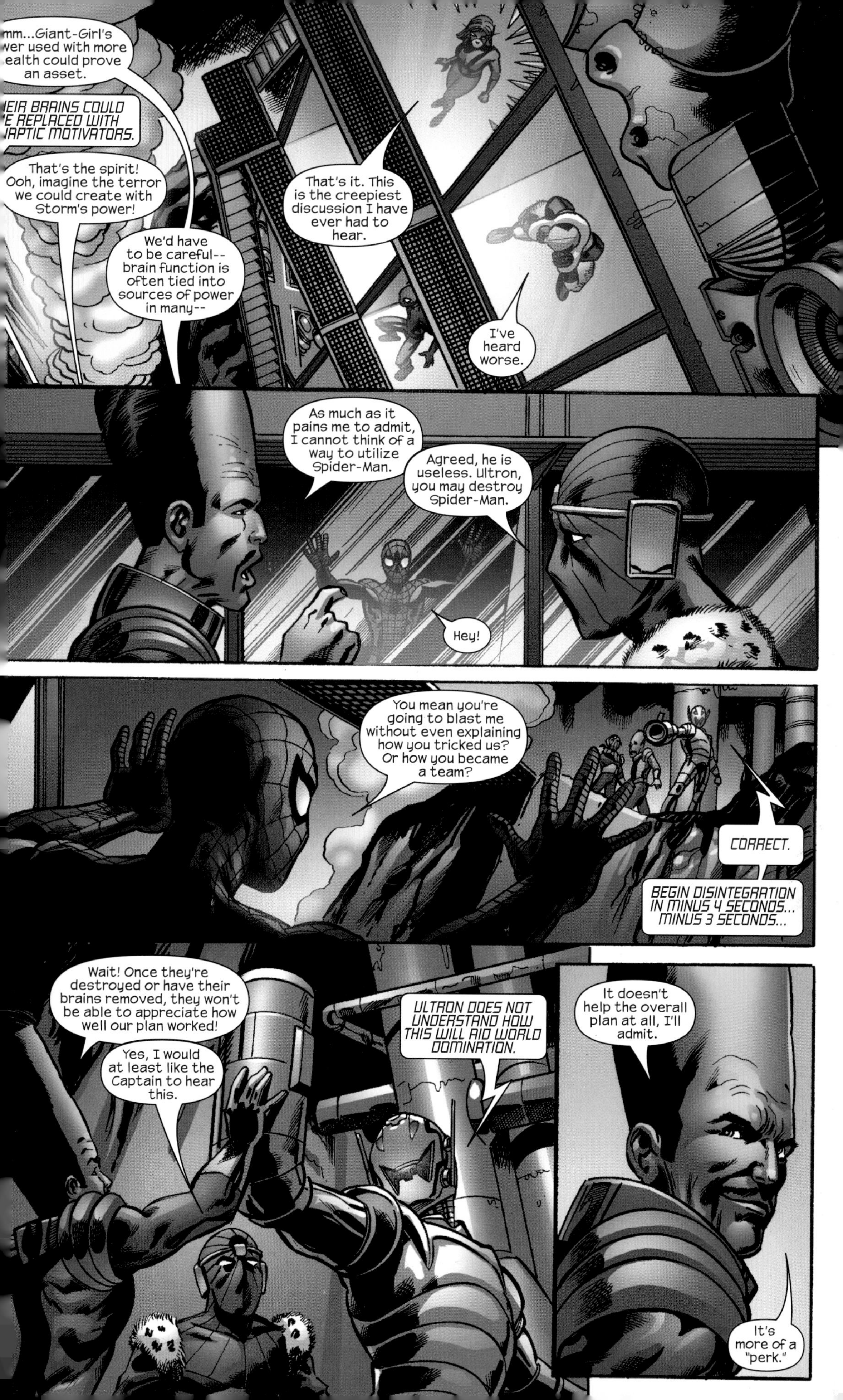

mm...Giant-Girl's
wer used with more
ealth could prove
an asset.
IEIR BRAINS COULD
E REPLACED WITH
IAPTIC MOTIVATORS.
That's the spirit! Ooh, imagine the terror we could create with Storm's power!
We'd have to be careful-- brain function is often tied into sources of power in many--
That's it. This is the creepiest discussion I have ever had to hear.
I've heard worse.
As much as it pains me to admit, I cannot think of a way to utilize Spider-Man.
Agreed, he is useless. Ultron, you may destroy Spider-Man.
Hey!
You mean you're going to blast me without even explaining how you tricked us? Or how you became a team?
CORRECT.
BEGIN DISINTEGRATION IN MINUS 4 SECONDS... MINUS 3 SECONDS...
Wait! Once they're destroyed or have their brains removed, they won't be able to appreciate how well our plan worked!
Yes, I would at least like the Captain to hear this.
ULTRON DOES NOT UNDERSTAND HOW THIS WILL AID WORLD DOMINATION.
It doesn't help the overall plan at all, I'll admit.
It's more of a "perk."

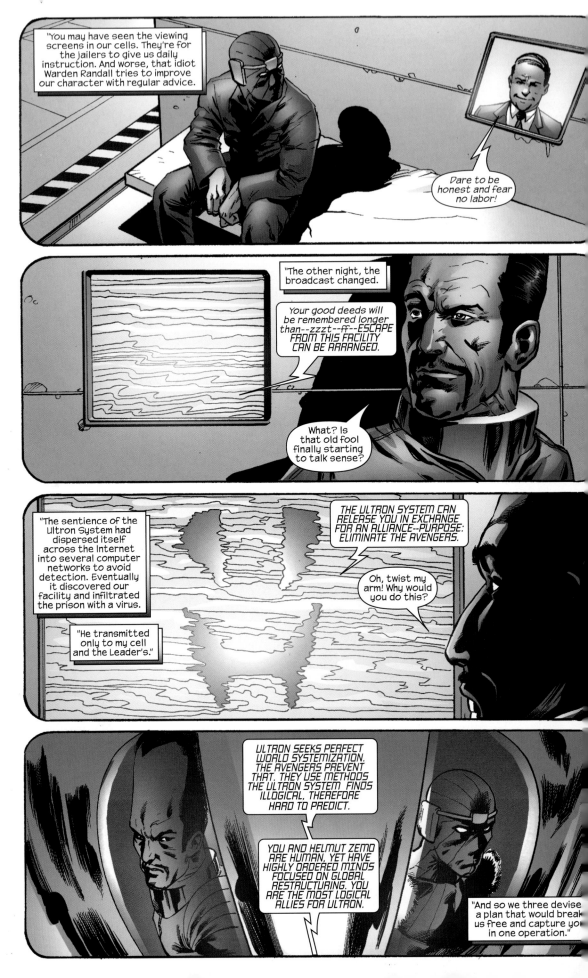

"You may have seen the viewing screens in our cells. They're for the jailers to give us daily instruction. And worse, that idiot Warden Randall tries to improve our character with regular advice."

Dare to be honest and fear no labor!

"The other night, the broadcast changed."

Your good deeds will be remembered longer than--zzzt--ff--ESCAPE FROM THIS FACILITY CAN BE ARRANGED.

What? Is that old fool finally starting to talk sense?

"The sentience of the Ultron System had dispersed itself across the Internet into several computer networks to avoid detection. Eventually it discovered our facility and infiltrated the prison with a virus."

"He transmitted only to my cell and the Leader's."

THE ULTRON SYSTEM CAN RELEASE YOU IN EXCHANGE FOR AN ALLIANCE--PURPOSE: ELIMINATE THE AVENGERS.

Oh, twist my arm! Why would you do this?

ULTRON SEEKS PERFECT WORLD SYSTEMIZATION. THE AVENGERS PREVENT THAT. THEY USE METHODS THE ULTRON SYSTEM FINDS ILLOGICAL, THEREFORE HARD TO PREDICT.

YOU AND HELMUT ZEMO ARE HUMAN, YET HAVE HIGHLY ORDERED MINDS FOCUSED ON GLOBAL RESTRUCTURING. YOU ARE THE MOST LOGICAL ALLIES FOR ULTRON.

"And so we three devise a plan that would break us free and capture you in one operation."

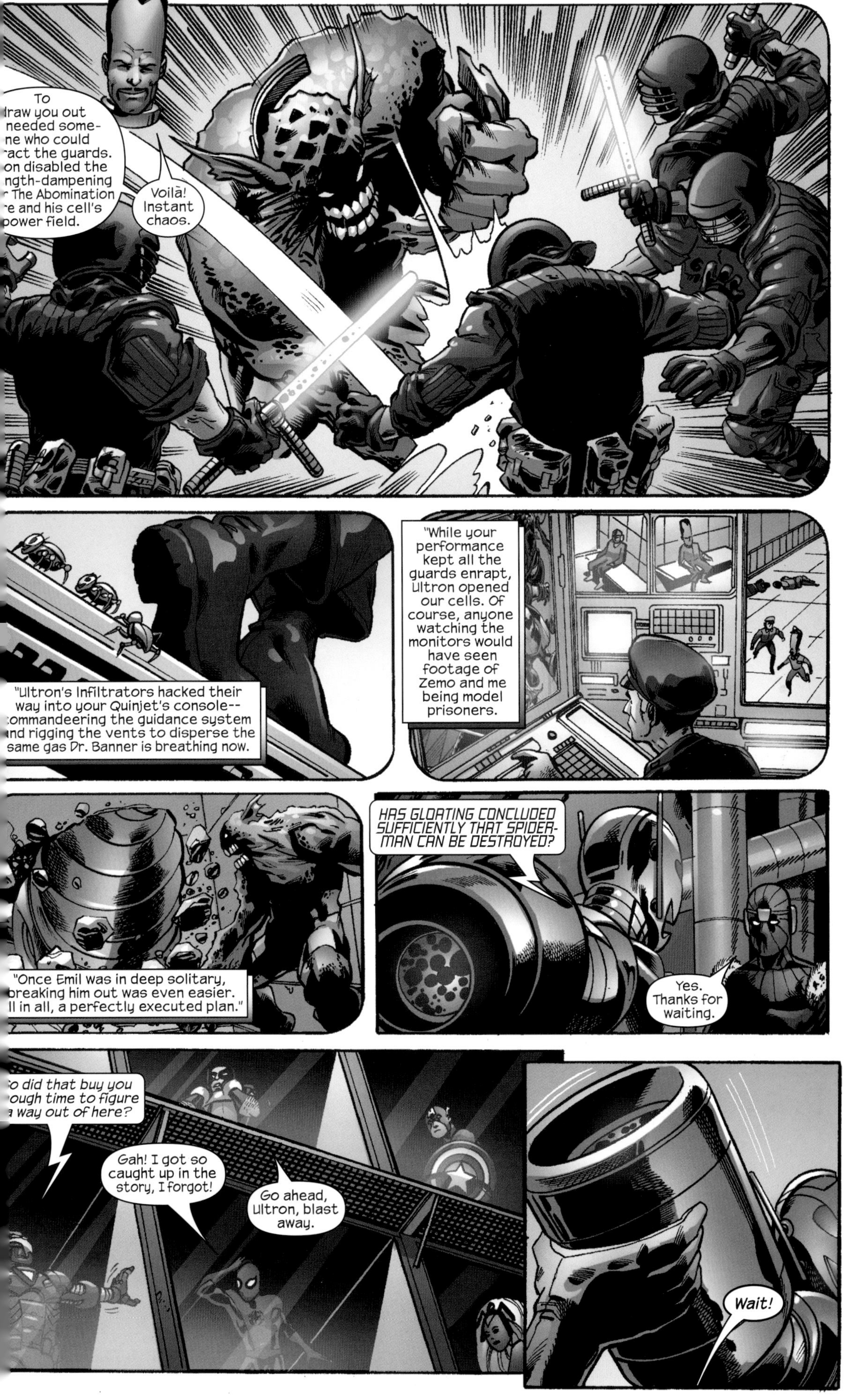

To
lraw you out
needed some-
ne who could
ract the guards.
on disabled the
ngth-dampening
r The Abomination
re and his cell's
power field.
Voilà! Instant chaos.
"Ultron's Infiltrators hacked their way into your Quinjet's console--
ommandeering the guidance system
nd rigging the vents to disperse the
same gas Dr. Banner is breathing now.
"While your performance kept all the guards enrapt, Ultron opened our cells. Of course, anyone watching the monitors would have seen footage of Zemo and me being model prisoners.
"Once Emil was in deep solitary,
breaking him out was even easier.
ll in all, a perfectly executed plan."
HAS GLOATING CONCLUDED SUFFICIENTLY THAT SPIDER-MAN CAN BE DESTROYED?
Yes. Thanks for waiting.
o did that buy you
ough time to figure
a way out of here?
Gah! I got so caught up in the story, I forgot!
Go ahead, Ultron, blast away.
Wait!

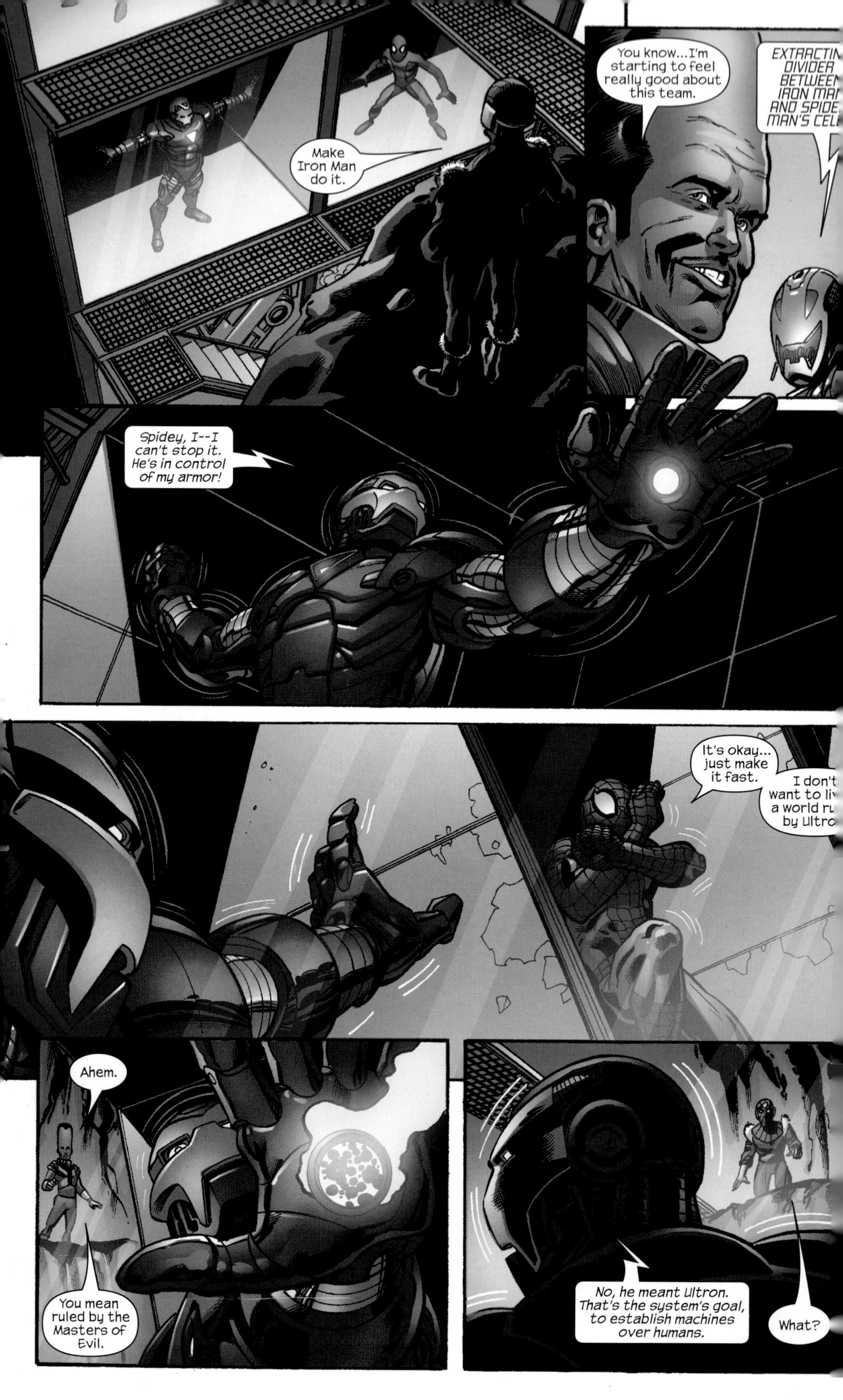

Make Iron Man do it.
You know...I'm starting to feel really good about this team.
EXTRACTIN DIVIDER BETWEEN IRON MAN AND SPIDE MAN'S CELL
Spidey, I--I can't stop it. He's in control of my armor!
It's okay... just make it fast.
I don't want to li a world ru by Ultro
Ahem.
You mean ruled by the Masters of Evil.
No, he meant Ultron. That's the system's goal, to establish machines over humans.
What?

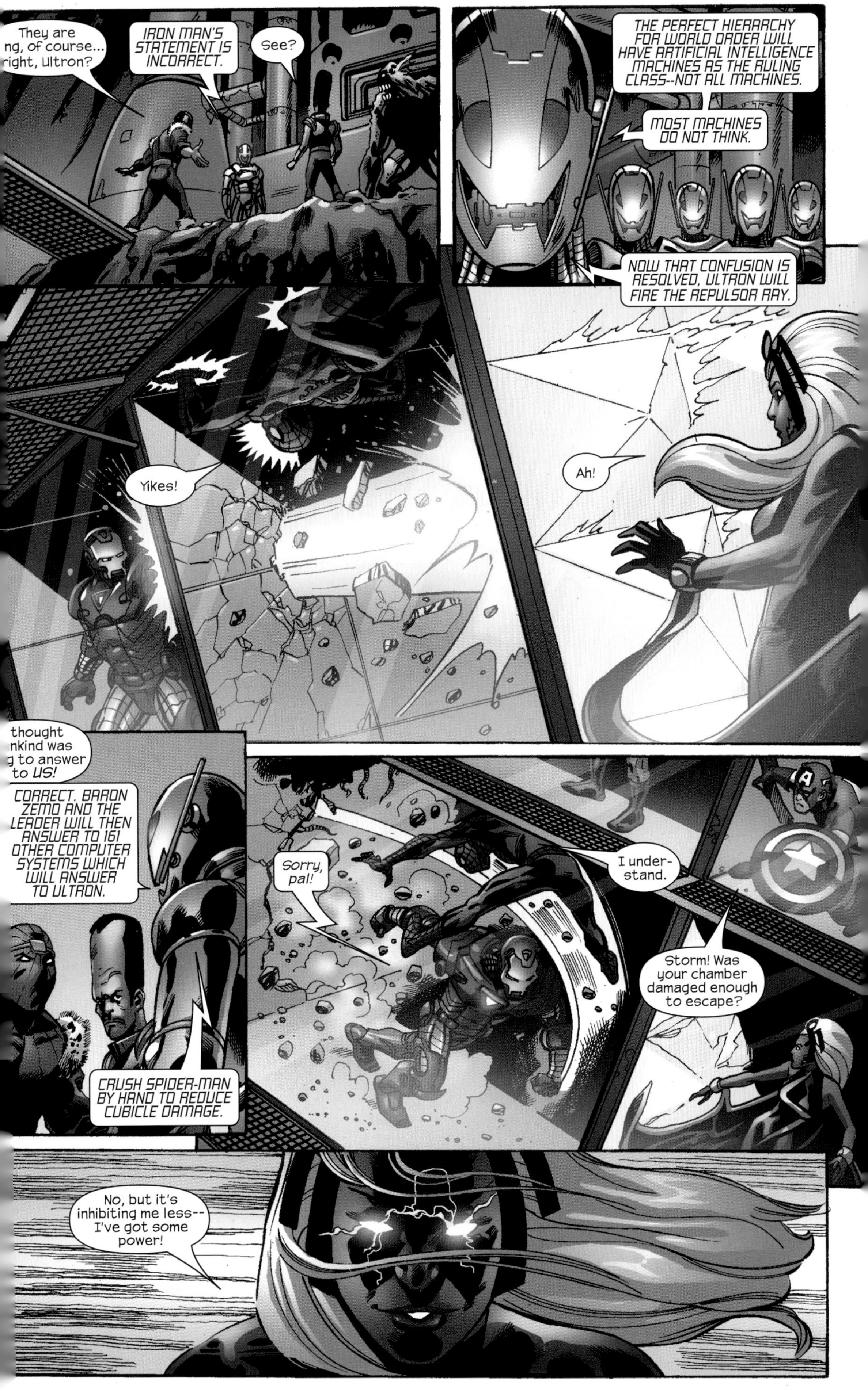
They are
ng, of course...
right, Ultron?
IRON MAN'S STATEMENT IS INCORRECT.
See?
THE PERFECT HIERARCHY FOR WORLD ORDER WILL HAVE ARTIFICIAL INTELLIGENCE MACHINES AS THE RULING CLASS--NOT ALL MACHINES.
MOST MACHINES DO NOT THINK.
NOW THAT CONFUSION IS RESOLVED, ULTRON WILL FIRE THE REPULSOR RAY.
Yikes!
Ah!
thought
nkind was
g to answer
to US!
CORRECT. BARON ZEMO AND THE LEADER WILL THEN ANSWER TO 161 OTHER COMPUTER SYSTEMS WHICH WILL ANSWER TO ULTRON.
CRUSH SPIDER-MAN BY HAND TO REDUCE CUBICLE DAMAGE.
Sorry, pal!
I understand.
Storm! Was your chamber damaged enough to escape?
No, but it's inhibiting me less-- I've got some power!

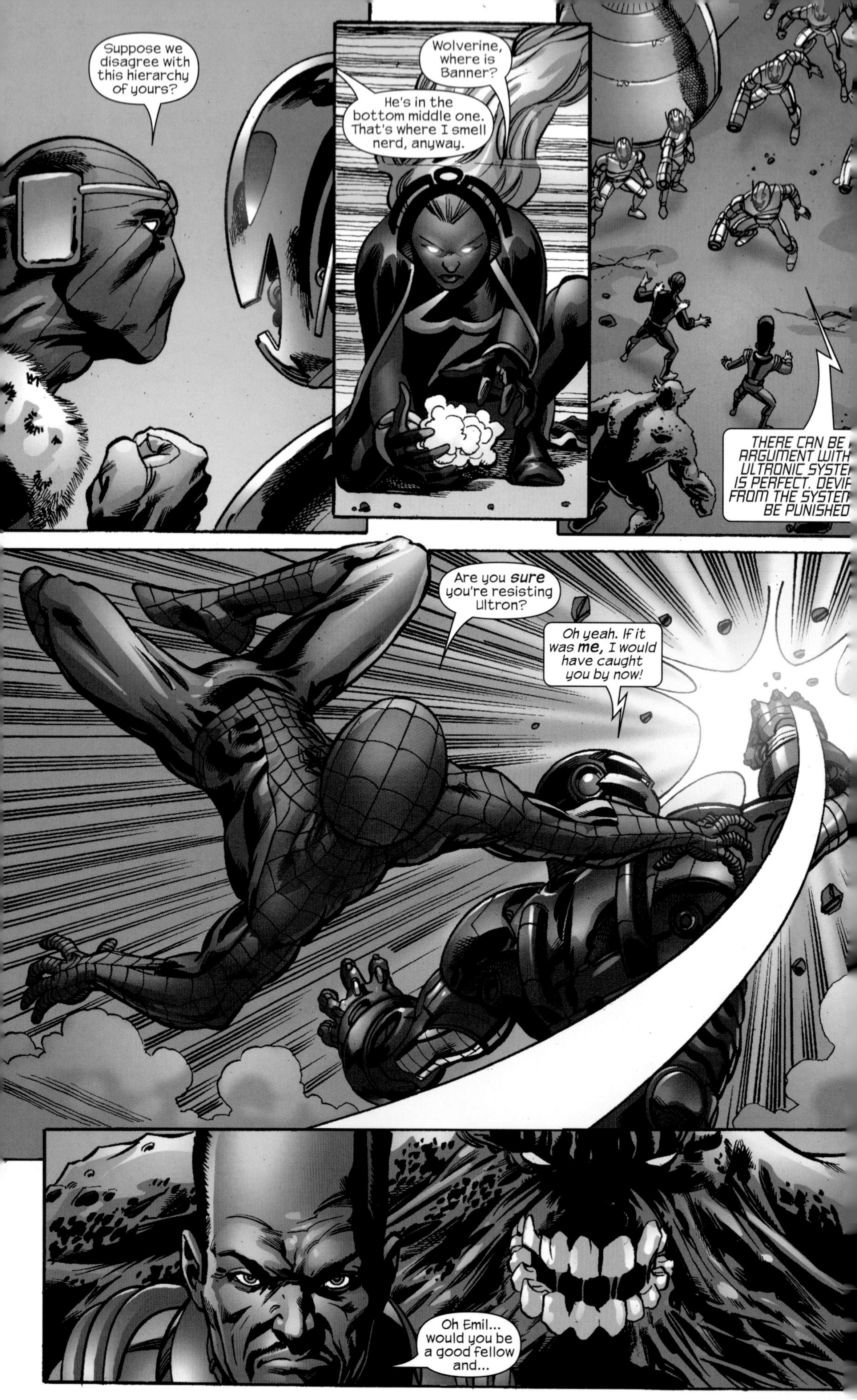
Suppose we disagree with this hierarchy of yours?
Wolverine, where is Banner?
He's in the bottom middle one. That's where I smell nerd, anyway.
THERE CAN BE
ARGUMENT WITH
ULTRONIC SYSTE
IS PERFECT. DEVI
FROM THE SYSTEM
BE PUNISHED
Are you *sure* you're resisting Ultron?
Oh yeah. If it was **me,** I would have caught you by now!
Oh Emil... would you be a good fellow and...

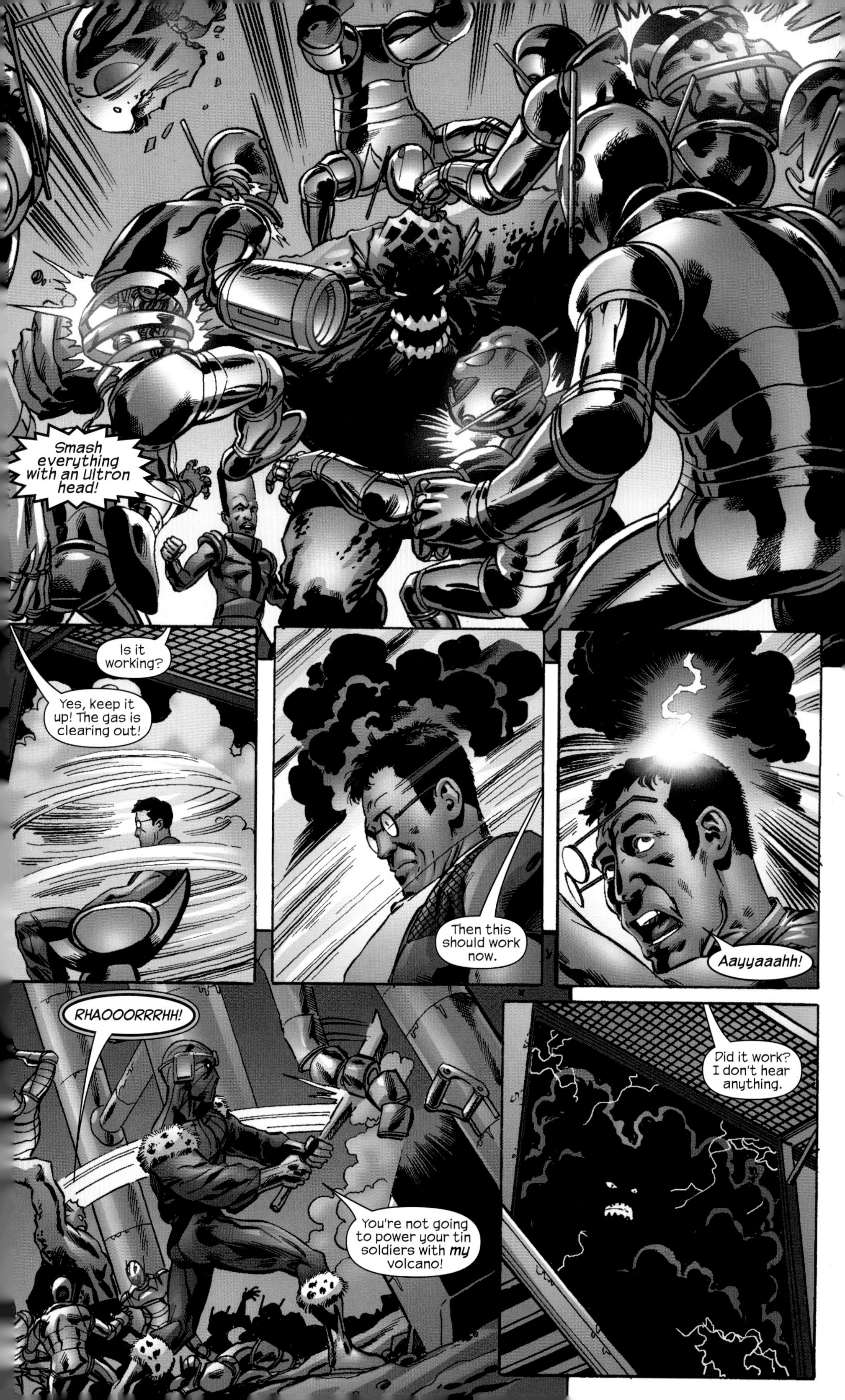
Smash everything with an Ultron head!
Is it working?
Yes, keep it up! The gas is clearing out!
Then this should work now.
Aayyaaahh!
RHAOOORRRHH!
You're not going to power your tin soldiers with *my* volcano!
Did it work? I don't hear anything.

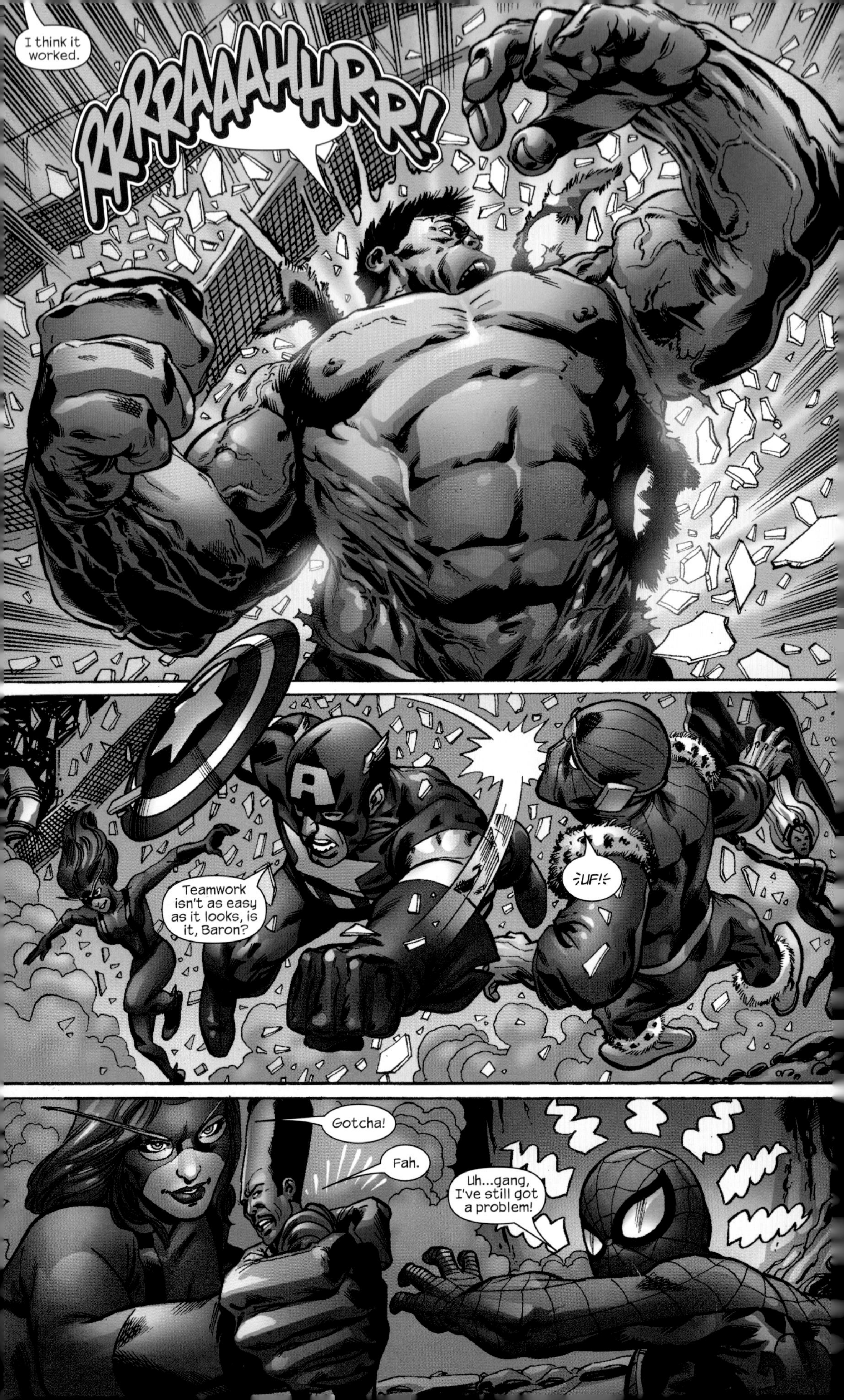
I think it worked.
RRRRAAAHHRRR!
Teamwork isn't as easy as it looks, is it, Baron?
UF!
Gotcha!
Fah.
Uh...gang, I've still got a problem!

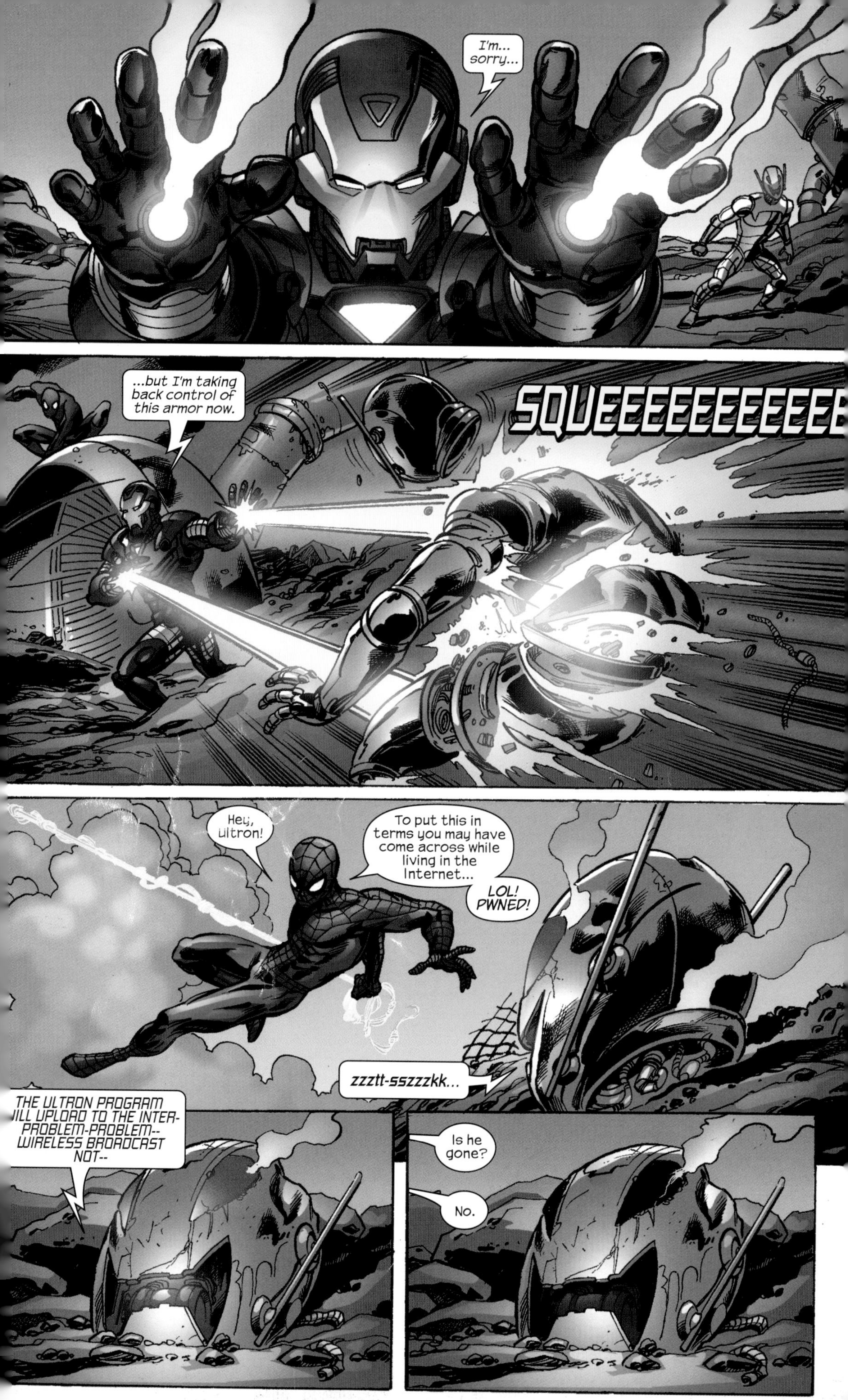
I'm... sorry...
...but I'm taking back control of this armor now.
SQUEEEEEEEEEEEEE
Hey, Ultron!
To put this in terms you may have come across while living in the Internet...
LOL! PWNED!
zzztt-sszzzkk...
THE ULTRON PROGRAM WILL UPLOAD TO THE INTER-PROBLEM-PROBLEM-- WIRELESS BROADCAST NOT--
Is he gone?
No.

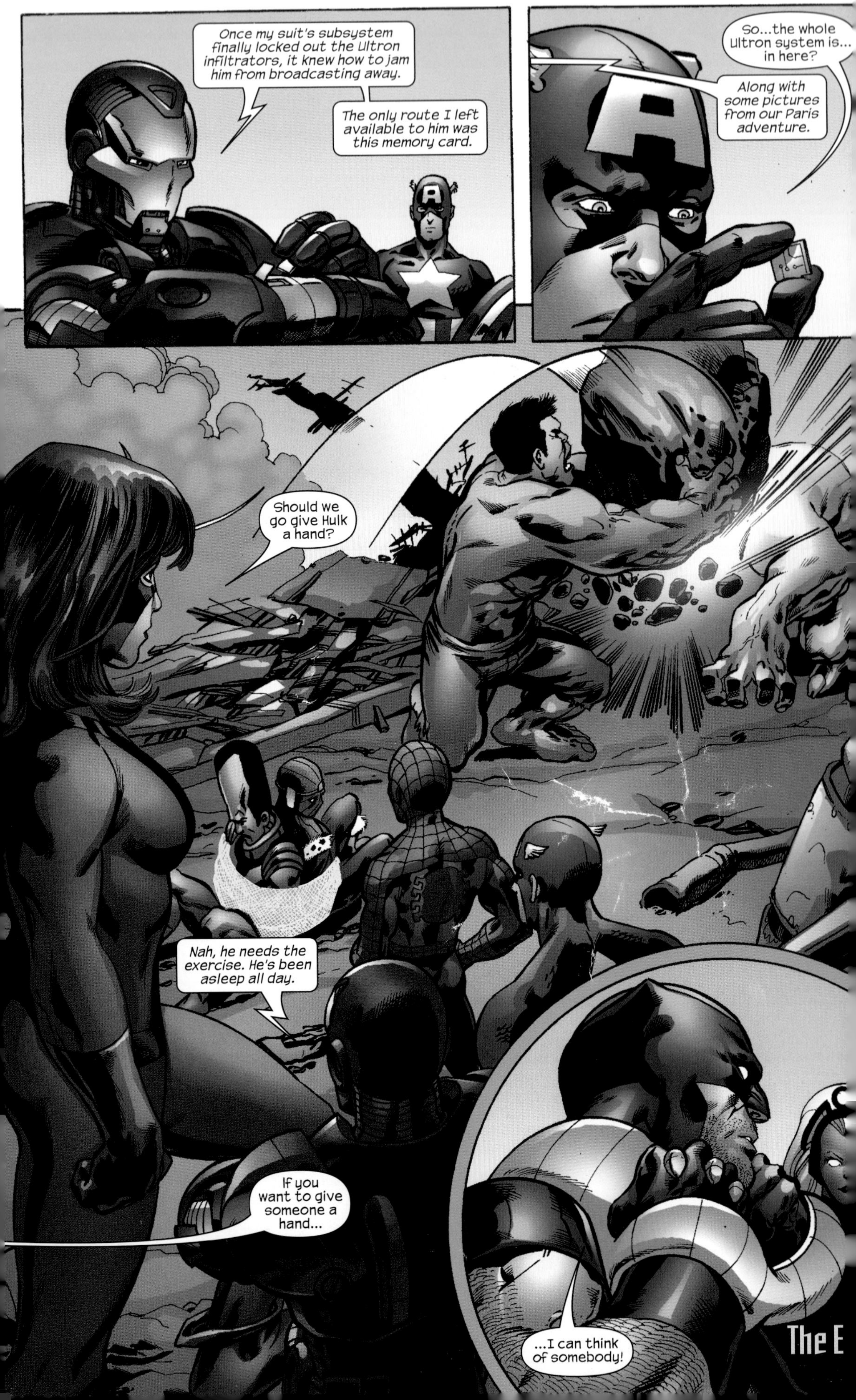
Once my suit's subsystem finally locked out the Ultron infiltrators, it knew how to jam him from broadcasting away.
The only route I left available to him was this memory card.
So...the whole Ultron system is... in here?
Along with some pictures from our Paris adventure.
Should we go give Hulk a hand?
Nah, he needs the exercise. He's been asleep all day.
If you want to give someone a hand...
...I can think of somebody!
The E